WHEN
THE RAINBOW
SNEEZED

Debbie E. Mills

ISBN: 1976577977
ISBN 13: 9781976577970
Library of Congress Control Number: 2017915089
CreateSpace Independent Publishing Platform
North Charleston, South Carolina

Stay loose for change.

~Thank You~

My sincere thank you to my loving family and friends. I am blessed to have lots of both and I appreciate you all.

I also thank my inner self for allowing me to be vulnerable enough to share some of my thoughts with the world.

Much love.

A DEDICATION STORY OF MY MOM AND DAD – MY BLESSINGS

My father, James Mills, left this earth at the young age of fifty-three. It seems that God made up the difference by keeping Mom alive... even after two major heart attacks. At least, that's one way I look at it. Being a baby boomer, many of my friends have neither parent living, so I am quite thankful for her to be here. My mother, Teresa Mills, is a delightful lady, and doesn't bite her tongue for anyone. Never has, and never will. Even

in her nineties, she will drop a one-liner
on you before you know it. She is known
for simply "telling it like it t-i is!" A very
balanced individual, she is smart, classy,
caring and humorous. Whatever task
is set before her, she completes it with
confidence. Mom is so comical; however,
I don't think she ever realizes it. Her
facial expressions and southern drawl
makes her delivery a hard act to follow.
Those who know her can easily relate.
She is a very fair-skinned woman with
beautiful hair and average in size.
Born and raised in the South, she
acquired a culinary expertise with an
unmistakable passion to craft perfect
recipes. All of her meals are made
from scratch and taste delicious.
Like most Southern cooks, when
you ask for the recipe, she replies, "a
pinch of this, and a dash of that."

I don't think anyone on the planet could ever fry chicken as good as her. No matter how busy she was, the taste of her chicken was always the same—perfect! In fact, it wasn't unusual for family and close friends to stop by our house with requests for her to fry chicken for a social event. It was that amazing. Mom loved to go to Las Vegas and play the slot machines. Most often, she would go on turn-around bus trips and return home early the next morning. She'd walk in the house with a touch of pewter still on the palms of her hands after handling all those silver dollars throughout the night. My siblings and I would ask her if she won, and it would tickle us when she'd start pulling those C notes out of her purse. Whipping hundred-dollar bills on the dining room table, one at a time, as she counted, "One, two, three, four!"

*It wasn't out of the norm for her
to win a few thousand dollars
on each one of these trips.*

*Now, if you really wanted to get
her upset, all you had to do was attempt
to bother her children. She would go to
bat for her kids and showered us with
love. Not only with hugs and kisses,
but with her tender loving care. She
provided strong love and protection
making sure we had the best. Like most
kids in our generation, we had chores.
Before doing anything in the kitchen,
we had to wash our hands. And, of
course, we always had to bless our food.
Mom was encouraging when it came
to us expressing our talents, and she
believed in academics. She also taught
us good morals, to get along with
others, and to have a grateful heart.*

Mom not only took great care of us, she loved caring for all children. She taught elementary school, and what stands out most is her deep commitment and compassion for others. I could easily see how much she cared for those who didn't have enough, whether food, clothing, or simply love and attention. It would not be unusual for me to come home from school and find a stranger (one of the kids from school) that she had brought home to bathe and dress in new clothes. She really felt for the kids who would be teased at school for poor hygiene, wearing torn or ill-fitting clothes or shoes, or for just having un-combed, unruly hair. She reached out to many, many children. Hopefully, they have or will pay it forward by having compassion and helping others. Mom enjoyed helping grown folks as well. When she was a social worker at DPSS, she made it her business to help those in need. It irritated her when co-workers took their time getting to their clients. She couldn't stand it when people needed food stamps and had to wait two weeks or so before they could receive them. She would do her best for her clients, and expedite the process as quickly as she could. Even though it might have not been company policy, I observed times when she gave personal loans to a few of her clients who were in desperate need. She would occasionally give a helping hand to those who didn't have transportation. Afterwork, she'd bring them home, feed them and then give them a ride home. She hated to see others do without, especially when it came to the basics, like food, shelter, and cleanliness. In many ways, the lyrics of Frank Sinatra's song, "I Did It My Way," reminds me so much of my mom. What immediately pops in my head is an instance that happened while she was employed at DPSS. She would leave home for work in the morning with a brown paper bag that carried her black cast iron skillet, potatoes, onions, a little oil, bacon, eggs and toast. Her co-workers would tell me how the aromas of perfectly cooked potatoes and onions would permeate throughout the building, causing everyone to stop their work and follow their nose to her desk. Of course, they would want a sample! Dad left us way too soon. Even though it has been forty-seven years since his death, at times, the scent of him is still present. Strange, but I do occasionally sense his presence. He was such a gentleman and gave Mom whatever she wanted, even when he didn't want to. He truly loved all his children and it was mutual. He was strong in his beliefs and didn't seem to desire much, other than to have a happy family. He was a true provider, working two and sometimes three jobs, so he could afford to give us the best. He was no nonsense though, and hated the use of curse words, especially around his kids. He wanted us all to stick together and get along, but of course, we had our fights as most kids do. Working as a Redcap at the Santa Fe Train Station in Pasadena, California, he was connected to many people, including celebrities. It was the way to travel in and out of the city for so many people back in the day. Having a train station in Pasadena is something that I truly miss. Dad would call my Mom and tell her to bring us kids down to the station *because certain celebrities were there, and we'd rush down to get an autograph. His work experience inspired my love for trains. Traveling by train was free for the family, and that's the way we traveled, whether it be to San Diego, Chicago, or Mississippi, a few of our regular destinations. We enjoyed the sleeper cars and all the sights along the way. The train is the perfect mode of transportation for those who enjoy the different sceneries it offers.*

I loved going to work with my father. Occasionally, I got to hang out with him on his workday. I remember things like putting pennies on the track and they'd get flattened out when the train ran over them, or getting my own Santa Fe tablets. My favorite was the chocolate bunnies at Easter time. Whenever the ears were broken during transit, they couldn't be

sold in the stores, so we got them free!
With the chocolate tasting just as good, we
had enough boxes of broken-eared bunny
rabbits for all of the kids on our street.
There's one thing that still sticks with
me about my father. When I was a
young girl, I would receive compliments
on my long hair or big brown eyes.
One day, dad sat me on his lap
and asked, "How much did you
have to pay to ride the bus?"
"Thirty-five cents." I replied.
He continued, "Regardless of how you
may look, or what you might have,
you'll always have to pay to ride like
everyone else." He said that no matter
how anyone looked, they had to pay
their fair share. He faithfully believed
that all people should be treated equal.
Being the excellent gardener that he was,
our yard was always manicured. Even the
bricks and rocks were always in perfect

place. He loved gardening. In fact, he found the work to be therapeutic and would hum or sing while he worked. Dad was also great at putting anything on the grill. In fact, one of my most pleasant childhood memories is of one of those summer days when Dad was grilling up some barbeque, and Mom was making homemade ice cream!

I was fortunate to have been raised by such great parents and to have grown up in a loving and caring environment, and I am forever grateful for it. ❤

WHEN THE RAINBOW SNEEZED

When the guests were singing in unison of the very last verse, "Hap-pee birth-daay tooo yoooou," I began to think about how truly blessed I am to have at least one of my parents still living. During the claps and cheers, I looked at the glow on Mom's face as she blew out her candles. I smiled and immediately told God how truly grateful I was to still have her with me and for continuing to shower her with His love.

We celebrated Mom's ninetieth birthday with all the bells and whistles, enjoying family and friends from near and far. Pink was my mother's favorite color. So of course, all of the decorations had a touch of rose in them. We were amazed as we watched the dusty, old-fashioned clubhouse transform into such a beautiful room. Everything in the room was pretty in pink, including the linens, balloons, utensils and beautiful blush-colored roses.

Mother had a pink corsage and wore a baby-soft pink, linen dress. She looked refreshingly beautiful. She knew it was her special day to shine and that she did! She shined like a diamond amongst her loved ones who were there to honor her.

It was a perfect day with live entertainment, great food, good people, and a full, open bar. What could possibly go wrong? Well, whenever alcohol is in the picture, there is a potential for chaos, and that's exactly what overshadowed the magnificence of this perfect celebration.

Mom's nephew, Malcolm McNeill, was in from Seattle. He is an extremely handsome guy in his mid-forties with premature salt and pepper, wavy locks. He was a sharp dresser and kept himself physically fit. He enjoyed his daily routine of hitting the gym. It would kill him to be caught looking out of shape. But with all that, his claim to fame was his perfect, pearly white teeth. He never wore braces, but you would bet money that he had. He believed that his smile was his ticket to anything in the world, and most of the time, it was.

Malcolm had great energy and left a great impression on every person he met. Although book smart, he was quite juvenile in his actions and often fell short when it came to common sense. About a month prior to Mom's birthday celebration, the family found out that Malcolm had been involved in a few misfortunes with the law. First, he was riding in a stolen car with a friend and got pulled over by the police. Then two weeks later, he was arrested for a DUI. Malcolm was a heavy drinker, so it was surprising that this was his first DUI.

Through the years, no matter where he'd been, he always managed to make it home safely. He didn't have a preference when it came to alcohol. He loved beer, whiskey or wine, all the same. Whenever you could catch Malcolm sober, he was the funniest and most charming person you'd ever want to meet. He's a phenomenal storyteller and has the memory of an elephant. There are full details in every story he tells and add that to his comical expressions and perfect timing, and you're in for a real treat.

Unfortunately, on the night of Mom's party Malcolm had too much to drink. He was in a conversation with a family friend, Chase Roberts, and to no surprise, the situation became volatile. Chase, who was White, was in his early thirties and grew up in the same neighborhood. Chase and Malcolm had been friends for many years. Our middle-class neighborhood was very diverse with a tinge of snootiness. Everyone got along extremely well. The tree-lined streets had homes with perfectly tended landscapes of St. Augustine grass and a variety of the most colorful flowers. Throughout the years, some of the connecting streets changed somewhat, but our block remained very nice.

Chase was a hippie type with long unkempt hair and a scruffy beard. He lived around the corner and his parents knew my parents, as well as Malcolm's. He was a casual guy and wouldn't harm a fly, even if the fly bit him—or at least that's how he was in his younger years. He was against any kind of confrontation because he came from a family who argued over anything and everything. They had more than enough in every category, except love. As Chase grew older, he seemed to lose his temper a lot quicker than usual. I imagine seeing his mother repeatedly being taken advantage of, could have possibly affected the change in his personality. A change that was becoming more noticeable.

He didn't particularly like being an only child. Often, he told his mother how much he would like to have a little brother or sister. Being alone was hard for him, especially when his parents had their confrontations. He wanted someone present, if no more than to help him cope with the pain. When he became frustrated, he would punch his pillows or cover his face to block out the sounds of his father yelling or his mother sobbing.

Having another child to help dis-
tract Chase from all the negativity would
have been in vain. In fact, his mother
didn't know how much longer she could
take the abuse. It was bad enough trying to raise one child on her own, let
alone have another. His mother did not
want any more children, not because
she wouldn't love them or couldn't afford them, but because of the ongoing
loveless relationship she had with her
husband.

Chase's father, Doug Roberts, was
a retired liquor salesman who had
started off small and built a successful
business into a very lucrative career.
He had been a well-known distribu-
tor who serviced many local stores, as
well as some of the hottest nightclubs
in Los Angeles. In his prime, he was
quite dapper and always had a way

with women. Besides being handsome, he always wore the best clothes, shoes and jewelry.

Having quite the reputation, whenever Doug stopped at one of the local clubs, women threw themselves at him. He had a great sense of humor and was extremely generous with his time and his money, and had a lot of both. However, he had his eyes on Nelda Price, Chase's mom. In fact, he met her at one of the nightclubs downtown. When he first laid eyes on her, he told his buddies that she was going to be his wife. Nelda was a respected journalist, who didn't frequent the nightclub scene. One night, she decided to go because her cousins were in town and wanted to party. If she had had it her way, she would have visited a museum or caught a movie. She was

not the partying type, and dreaded going, but didn't want to disappoint her
guests. She would much rather enjoy a
discussion about politics or be in the
kitchen baking cookies from her great
grandmother's recipe book.

It's often said that opposites at-
tract and Nelda was indeed quite the
opposite of Doug, who was the flashy
type. She dressed very plainly and
had a quiet disposition. Nelda enjoyed
reading and belonged to two book
clubs. She ended up giving Doug her
phone number and they became good
friends. They eventually dated, got
married and had a good relationship
for several years. Unfortunately, as the
years passed, their relationship shifted
for the worse.

Doug began working extremely
long hours and occasionally didn't

return home at night. As he made liquor deliveries to the nightclubs, he began to have a drink or two, or sometimes three or four, which led to dancing and flirting with the ladies. A few times, he would leave home on a Friday and not see or talk to Nelda for a couple of days. She always asked him to give her phone call here and there so that she wouldn't worry about him, but he never did. Nelda knew something was going on, but whenever she questioned Doug, he wouldn't give her a straight answer. Instead, he would avoid the situation by taking her out to a fancy restaurant or buying her something special.

Nelda was book smart, but not at all street smart. However, she knew her marriage was on the rocks. One night she followed her intuition and went to one of the local nightclubs. She ordered a glass of wine and sat at one of the tables in the back of the room. She sat there and observed all the men and women—talking, laughing, hugging, kissing, and dancing.

Even though they seemed to be enjoying themselves, she thought, "What a waste of time!"

She took a sip of her red wine and as her eyes scanned the area, she almost choked because of what she saw. There was Doug and some woman on the dance floor! Doug had great rhythm and was an excellent dancer, and he knew it. When the song ended, he graciously escorted the lady back to her table. Nelda is eyeing him the whole time, watching him flirt with the ladies and then shoot the breeze with the guys. He seemed to be having a ball! Nelda began to think that maybe she was interfering with his business, and pleasure for that matter, but she also believed that since she was his wife, she could spy on him if she wanted to. Eventually, Doug went over to the bar to order a new drink.

Nelda softly walked up to him and said, "Excuse me, but what are you doing here? It doesn't look like you are working at all!"

Doug's eyes became as big as saucers and he whipped back, "What are *you* doing here?"

Nelda swiftly turned away and walked out of the club, just as quietly as she came in.

Luckily for Doug, she is not the type to make a big scene. Nelda was a woman of class and would never create a scene in public...especially over a man, even if it was her husband.

That incident never surfaced again, but Doug continued to do whatever he wanted until he retired. By then, he drank vodka every day which made him very confrontational and sometimes abusive. Nelda struggled in every aspect of her marriage because respect simply didn't exist. She didn't want to end her marriage, though, at least not yet.

It hurt Chase to see his mother overpowered, so much that he became bitter about it. He felt that there was nothing he could do to protect himself or his mom, and it was obvious that they were both afraid. This resulted in him holding an obvious grudge against his father.

Chase would dislike his own favorite color of red at times, because of the

negative reminder it could give. It wasn't
unusual for him to come home to see
a dozen red roses on the dining room
table with a note from his father to his
mother, apologizing for his ill behavior.
Unfortunately, the flowers always had a
bitter reminder to him of what his mom
endured. That bitterness seemed to fil-
ter into his sub-consciousness, more
times than not. In spite of it all, he continued to collect lots of red items, such
as caps, jackets, and shoes - he even had
a red piano!

Chase always thought that his father was jealous of him because he
was a momma's boy. He also believed
his father was disappointed with him
since he didn't finish college. Doug
wanted his son to get a good educa-
tion, especially since he didn't get
one. In the middle of his sophomore
year, Chase realized that he had

more of a creative mindset than an academic one, therefore, his desire to finish school seemed to diminish a bit each semester. It soon became a struggle for him to go to school. Chase loved all of the arts, and he could paint landscapes just as well as he could sing and play the piano. He was a true artist.

Hanging out with all sorts of artists, from painters, to poets, to musicians, Chase finally stopped going to school altogether and joined a band. Most of the band members were pretty cool. However, every now and then, they would run across a knucklehead who had to be replaced because of heavy drug and alcohol use. Sadly, this was the norm for some of the greatest artists of all time and cost many of them their lives.

Chase had a way with words and a voice that had a smooth delivery, like Michael Franks or Bobby Caldwell. Sometimes he would do a poetry selection while playing guitar or piano softly in the background. He was mesmerizing and audiences always gave him a standing ovation.

He was quite talented and was better than average on most any instrument. He loved performing at various hole in the wall joints throughout Los Angeles. The kind of venues that allowed him to take a few tokes from a cigarette or blunt, or a sip from his Hennessey in-between his words. The more he hit and sipped, the smoother he delivered his message, which was always inspiring.

Chase felt that the anger his father had for him was taken out on his mother and he was filled with guilt about this. He loved his mother and was sorry that she endured such a painful marriage. As early as he can remember, he and his mother had always been close, much closer than he and his father. He built a bond early on with his mother and he remembered everything from his childhood, which he enjoyed. He and his mom would do special things together like go to the park on a hot summer day and get ice cream. Sometimes, they would ride bikes to the neighborhood market to pick up groceries. Chase loved it when his mom put some of the groceries in his basket to carry back home. It made him feel like he was doing his share.

The meals that they cooked together were also memorable. Chase

was intrigued about cooking and ended up creating lots of his own original
dishes. He enjoyed watching his mother in the kitchen, and many times she
allowed him to stir, mix or crumble
crackers for meat loaf or other dishes
that required breadcrumbs. It made
him feel like he was really helping her.
He loved to smash up crackers with
his little fists, as if he they were army
tanks. To say the least, Chase has fond
memories of his mother and wished
there was something he could do to
protect her.

Chase witnessed his father mis-
treating his mother, until she finally
divorced him after thirty-two years of
marriage. Even though he was happy
for his mother, the divorce affected
Chase negatively in many ways. He became easily agitated over little things

and his mood was usually down. He was less concerned about pleasing people, going places or doing things, almost to the point of slight depression.

Plus, Chase vowed that he would never, ever marry… and to date, he hasn't. His parent's relationship certainly tainted his thoughts around dating and romance. Whenever his relationships became too serious, he would end it with one senseless reason or another. He became quite an expert at starting an argument out of nowhere, just for the sake of ending the relationship. Truly a loss because deepdown, Chase is a caring person and would probably make a great husband and father.

Chase's friend, Malcolm, had a great job at a well-established computer company in Los Angeles. However, as the economy changed so did the company's direction, shifting potential business and profits to the Seattle area. Malcolm was offered a substantial relocation package and without hesitation, he took it. He figured, what the heck, he had nothing to lose. He and his wife had separated and since his son, Joel, was out of the house, he could call his own shots.

Joel had moved to Washington, DC, where he finished college and always told Malcolm, "Dad, don't live your life based on me because I'm all grown up now. I'll make my own decisions and when I make a mistake, I'll figure out what to do on my own. If I need you, I'll call you."

Joel ended up loving the East Coast and decided to stay there after meeting and falling in love with his fiancé, Kathi Coleman. Joel landed a great job as senior accountant at one of the largest accounting firms in DC. With his knowledge and personality, he was well on his way up the corporate ladder. He loved his Dad and thanked him for kicking him out of the nest early because it helped to make him a responsible and productive individual. He had no idea of the animosity going on between his Dad and his life-long friend, Chase. If he had, he would be heartbroken because Chase was like an uncle to him. They had a special bond.

Malcolm was quite impressed with Joel and how he tackled the world without any inhibition. He was thankful that his son was so motivated, and that he wanted to make something of himself. Joel was never spoiled. Malcolm always told him that he had to work for what he wanted in life, because that's what he had to do. He didn't believe in handing him something for nothing. Joel believed that in life, "You get back what you put in."

So far, Malcolm loved Seattle and always spoke about how the air quality is so much better than that in Southern California. When he first moved to Seattle, he and Chase kept in touch via email and phone calls. In fact, he invited Chase to come up a few times to visit and would introduce him to his buddies at the different jazz clubs. Malcolm knew most of the cool spots and the owners, respectively. Whenever possible, Malcolm would ask the manager if Chase could do a quick performance during intermission, or warm up the crowd for the headliner.

Quite often, he received an expected "yes!"

Chase loved it whenever he got a chance to do his thing, especially while on vacation. It seemed like he performed even greater whenever he was away from his home base. He would get a kick out of working the crowd, letting them know that he was visiting from out of town and invited them to come to one of his shows in Los Angeles. He always announced his schedule first, so that folks could easily lookup his performance dates on his calendar. Chase loved Seattle and visited there quite often. However, as time passed, Chase and Malcolm were out of touch for long periods of

time. No matter what, they were buddies and always picked up where they
left off.

THE PARTY WAS ON

The guests really enjoyed themselves at Mom's party. A lot of family (and friends) hadn't seen each other in years and the ages ranged from ninety to Mom's great, great, great-granddaughter, Meela, who was only nine months old. It was good to see that our family was starting to grow some.

The blenders were going and the drinks were being poured. Off to the side of the main party room, a few tables were set up so the bid whiz and domino players could get down. The real fun of both games, besides the challenge of winning, is that the players talk a lot of smack. It was Mom's day and she really enjoyed playing cards.

We were all in awe that she could still remember how to shuffle the cards, deal, and most surprising of all, bid her hand! Mom was a good whiz player, but she hated to lose and would sometimes out bid her opponent just so she could have the bid. She would hardly ever let anyone run a Boston on her (which means the opposing team wins all the books). Whenever it looked like she was headed to Boston, on the last book she would accidentally drop a card under the table on purpose.

Then, she would shout out "Misdeal!"

I caught her in the act once, which she replied with, "Shhhh."

Chase and Malcolm were caught up in conversation with a few other guys, just shootin' the breeze, doing a lot of bragging and crumbing, like guys do.

Every now and then, there were loud bursts of laughter, preceded by an "Ah man...you got me," or "that was a good one."

The guys were really having a good time, up until when Chase made the mistake of telling a joke about slavery that Malcolm didn't quite appreciate. Some of the other guys didn't like it either, but no one else make a big stink about it like Malcolm did.

The joke didn't sit well with him at all. It affected Malcolm in the worse way, and his attitude and facial expression made it obvious. Even though Chase didn't mean any harm, he had a careless attitude about it, which made matters even worse. Malcolm took everything the wrong way. He expressed a few unpleasant words to Chase and when he did, Chase unexpectedly slid into a combative mode. What started out as normal, fun, conversation swiftly turned sour. The language from both men became increasingly loud and rude.

Malcolm was very serious when it came to his heritage and felt that it is a real privilege to be Black. He felt that Blacks are the strongest of all races and that made him proud. He was bitter about how his race was mistreated during slavery, and how, even today, there are educated people like him who must go an extra mile just to break even.

When Chase finished the last line of his joke, Malcolm told him that "he didn't think it was funny at all."

In fact, Malcolm believed that Chase had disrespected every Black person who existed, including those at the party, which was about eighty-five percent of the guests.

Chase replied, "It's only a joke, man. It's not my fault that history is the way it is. I didn't have anything to do with slavery."

But, just as Chase got the last syllable of the last word out, BAM! Malcolm socked him in the jaw as hard as he could. It was as if he was going for a knockout punch in the last round of the last fight in his life. You could see Chase's face instantly swell with redness. His sunglasses went one way, his cigar and his red hat flew off in another, and he tumbled to the ground.

Both men tangled up violently across the perfectly green lawn just outside the clubhouse. As they scuffled like teenagers, one of the neighbors called the police. They quickly arrived and took them book into custody.

When the officer asked, "What happened?"

Chase yelled, "Malcolm started it!"

Malcolm shouted back at Chase, "You started it man with your snide remarks, but trust and believe that I'm not done with you. I can't wait to get a hold of you again and when I do, hopefully, there won't be any one around to break us up... I'm going to finish you off!"

Since there was such a large area
around the clubhouse, no one even
noticed that the ill-fated incident took
place. A couple of neighbors took note
of the police car, but they didn't as-
sociate it to the party. Obviously, they
thought they were there for something else and never realized two of
the guests at the party had just been
removed from the premises.

Later that day, Malcolm and Chase
were eventually released from jail and
both were still very angry, and it was obvious that they weren't ready to forgive
each other. In fact, they never got over
it. Each went their separate way and,
unintentionally, started a race war.

As Chase told his side of the story,
his family and friends became bitter
and hateful toward Blacks. In turn,
when Malcolm related his thoughts

about the incident, his family and circle of friends became enraged toward Whites. Neither of the guys were racist, but perhaps, slightly prejudice when it came to protecting their relatives. This may be a prejudice that lives within everyone. I think most of us hate to see anyone hurt, especially our own.

Chase's first cousin, Michael Peters, had always felt that there was an imbalance as far as races were concerned. He didn't appreciate seeing his cousin all beat up. He told Chase that they should find Malcolm and kick his butt, and the sooner the better, because he could barely stomach what had happened.

Michael's past was nothing to be desired. He always seemed to meet up with the wrong group of people and his peers were in and out of trouble on the regular. When he was in his mid-twenties, he met Corina Riley, a small, but bossy girl who had three big brothers who always backed her up, right or wrong.

Corina loved dyeing her hair soft hues of pink, blue and purple, and wore it all tousled up under a baseball cap that read "Flawless" across the front. Surprisingly, her hair looked fashionably nice and she always received compliments and questions about it. She was extremely creative and expressed it on her tatted arms and diamond piercings on her nose. She appeared to be a wannabe tomboy, but was actually quite pretty. She wore a ring on every finger except her thumbs and her core wardrobe consisted of torn jeans, tight fitted t-shirts and tennis shoes.

34

Her jeans were always ironed and her shoes perfectly matched her nail polish and whatever cap she wore on any given day. Corina kept a blunt behind her right ear. She would never be caught without wearing her blue-colored round sunglasses. Even on cloudy days, she would still be sporting those shades.

Corina's brothers loved their little sister and didn't allow anyone to mess with her, which kept a lot of boys from dating her. When Michael met Corina, he was unaware of her brothers and by the time he met them, he and Corina had already been dating and fell in love. Sadly, they fell for all the wrong reasons.

Her brothers welcomed Michael, but also warned him that he better treat their sister right, or he would be

six feet under. He assured them that
he would, particularly since he truly
loved Corina, even though she introduced him to drugs and gangs. Her
brothers were in gangs and on drugs
as well. It was as if Michael didn't have
a chance.

He became deeply involved with
one of the largest gangs in Southern
California. In fact, he was one of the
top commanders which made Corina
proud. It made her feel powerful that
her man was so highly ranked in such a
treacherous group.

Michael was now doing malicious
acts toward the young and the elderly.
Whenever he wanted to, he would com-
mand his members to do wrong. They
would steal purses from older women
and kidnap younger women to control
them. They also got into fistfights and

it was nothing for Michael to pop a few caps into someone's butt.

Michael was always on the run from something or somebody. He wanted to do damage on a larger scale though. He had always believed that Whites were over and above all other races, especially Blacks. He was willful and ill-tempered and his buddies were the same. Now that the attention was brought to him, he felt that Blacks were advancing up the corporate ladder too fast anyway. His thoughts about racism grew and helped him to grow a bad attitude.

This incident with Chase and Malcolm pushed Michael over the edge. His thoughts were that the White race was accustomed to being on top of world, running ninety percent of corporate businesses, sports,

and entertainment, basically everything. He also felt that it was expected
that Whites should hold high-level po-
sitions, such as presidents, vice presidents, CEOs, and the like.

To have had a Black president run
this country was just way out of line
in his mind. He thought that Whites
always needed to be the leaders, and
what a misfortune it was when they
had to give up eight years to former
president Barack Obama.

Michael put it in Chase's mind that
maybe there should be a separation
between all races. Although Chase
wasn't a racist per se, listening to his
cousin made him happy to be White.
Not only because it made him feel
safe, it made him feel superior. One
thing that is puzzling is that Chase
never faced any racial issue like this

before. On the contrary, he's always been a person who got along with everybody. He always had friends of many nationalities and even played music in multicultural bands. The incident with Malcolm and Chase was a real game changer for both men.

Malcolm had already made Chase feel bad when he punched him in the face several times, which bruised him up badly. He was embarrassed, but most of all he lost respect for Malcolm. Since that day, things were never the same between the two, their relationship was just as bruised as Chase's face, to say the least.

Malcolm was very familiar with various groups of freedom fighters who were simply sick and tired of being sick and tired: organizations like the NAACP, The Black Panthers, SNCC, and others. He knew that Black people were done with the slave jokes, period. They were also tired being held back because of the color of their skin, not being promoted fairly, or in the worst cases, innocent lives taken for no apparent reason. They had heard enough of Blacks being "in the wrong place at the wrong time" and accepting that phrase as a legitimate and final answer. Blacks have had enough of hatred poured on them from the beginning of time. In some instances, it appears that times are changing for the better economically, only to hear heart-breaking news of another Black family dealing with a wrongful death, or another child killed from gang violence.

Well, so much for times getting better. In speculation, we have songs etched in our mind like, "Keep On Pushing," Curtis Mayfield, "What's Going On?", Marvin Gaye, and "A Change is Gonna Come," Sam Cooke.

PARTY ON, PARTY STRONG

Other than Malcolm and Chase's unpleasant issue at Mom's party, the rest of the day and night went well. The live entertainment was enjoyable. People kicked back and relaxed on the smooth jazz songs, and were up on the dance floor when the funky R&B songs blasted through the speakers. It was heartfelt to see so many people shaking their bodies and enjoying themselves. Big, little, old and young, they were all having a fun time. The musicians were great and played all the old-school music. If you could name it, they could play it!

As the night was winding down, close friends offered to help me clean up the clubhouse and we cleared the tables and emptied the trash. Others collected flowers and centerpieces, and since we had so many beautiful flowers, I suggested that people take some home. There were also cases of red and white wine that hadn't been opened, so I gave each guest a bottle as a 'thank you' for attending. We left the place just like we found it…spotless!

As the time had finally wound down, I began to get Mom ready to go back to her health care facility. It took special attention to get her in and out of the car, and I knew just how to handle her without hurting anyone in the process. Even though Mom wasn't a big woman, she was still quite heavy. She had to be lifted and carried just right or you could possibly get a back injury. One incorrect twist or turn could be devastating.

Everyone was totally exhausted. It was a very nice, but extremely long day and it showed on Mom's face. We knew that it was well past her bedtime, but it was well worth staying up late. Once I got her back to the facility, she could hit the sack.

When I opened the car door to put Mom in, Goldie (my cute Maltipoo) quickly hopped up on the seat without any hesitation at all.

There she sat, wagging her tail while happily waiting for the car to crank up. The folks at Mom's facility love Goldie. In fact, everyone who meets her loves her. Whenever I visit Mom without her, all the residents would ask "Where is Goldie?" She is good therapy for the residents, because the sight of her seems to bubble them up with happiness. The workers at the health facility are good to Mom. Many of them often mention how much fun she is, even when she's trying to be fussy. The workers laugh with her in a caring way because they know she never means any real harm.

I waited outside Mom's room while the CNA helped to her get ready for bed. After a few minutes, she waved her hand me, letting me know that Mom was snug as a bug and all ready to retire for the night. I walked in the room and I told Mom how much I enjoyed her special day and how great it was for our family and friends to come together to honor her. Mom smiled at me and thanked all of us for such a wonderful birthday celebration. She mentioned how elated she was to see so many people that she hadn't seen in years.

Before I left the room, Mom pulled me down close to her chest, kissed me on the cheek, and whispered, "I love you and I am so thankful to have you as my daughter."

I replied, "Thank you Mom, I love you back, and God couldn't have given me a better Mother. You had a long day, Mama, so get some rest."

"I will...good night," she said.

"Good night and don't forget to say your prayers," I replied as I turned off her light and headed home.

REFLECTION...REFRESH

I woke up feeling like most of my energy had already been robbed. It seemed like it was around 11:00am, but it was only 9:00! I finally got up out of bed, gave thanks for the new day and began to move forward. As I washed my body from the pros and cons of yesterday, I felt refreshed. The warm suds were especially relaxing as

I lathered my skin with subtle scents of Frankincense and Myrrh. "Mmm," I said under my breath, "this stuff smells so good!" If no one else was there to witness how wonderful it smelled, at least I was.

As the soap and water ran down my back, thoughts of Chase and Malcolm came to the forefront of my mind. While it was just a few days ago, their ugly incident played like a video running in my head.

"I can't believe that they were out there in public, acting like immature teenagers," I repeated loudly in my mind.

They ought to be ashamed of themselves, but I bet that they aren't even thinking about what happened, so neither should I. Nonetheless, I just could not believe how they tainted such a good friendship. It was one thing to have an argument, but to get into an actual fistfight and have the police haul them away was just too much. One positive aspect of the situation is that they didn't ruin Mom's party. Had that happened, I would probably never speak to either one of them... never, ever again.

I got dressed, put on a touch of makeup, brushed my hair, and then headed downstairs to get the coffee percolating. I opened my shutters, and the front door, and realized what a gorgeous day it was! The sun brightened the entire first floor of my home. The temperature was hitting around seventy-two degrees, paired with a tad bit of a breeze. I've always loved the morning air because it usually smells so fresh, especially near the canyons.

Clean and fresh, but lasts only up until all the cars crank up and pollute the air with horrible toxins from their smoky tailpipes. Nevertheless, the air was still much better than a lot of places in Southern California.

Turkey bacon is a mainstay in my house and I quickly cooked two pieces and buttered a slice of toasted sprouted bread. I usually add egg whites, but this particular morning I thought I'd pass. In-between preparing my breakfast, I changed Goldie's water and gave her a couple of doggie biscuits. Whenever I eat she's there eyeing my food, so I make it her feeding time as well.

I decided to sit outside, enjoy my breakfast, and sip on my mimosa while thinking of my plans for the day. I had just finished my last bite of toast when my phone rang. It was my neighbor, Charlene Stratton. She was such a great neighbor. When I first moved to the area, she and her husband, Ray, welcomed me with open arms. She's the type of neighbor that if she gets wind that I'm feeling under the weather, I can expect her to ring my doorbell to hand me a bowl of homemade chicken noodle soup. She is an excellent cook and everything she makes is homemade. She even grows her own herbs and spices and would occasionally hand me a bunch of fresh basil or rosemary. She invites me to many events and I always have a great time in her company.

Charlene asked, "Are you watching CNN?"

I replied, "Uh, no. I'm out on the patio just finishing breakfast."

She then said, "Well, turn it on when you get back in the house… there's some really crazy and scary stuff going on." I quickly ran inside and turned to CNN and saw ….Breaking News….Student goes on shooting binge, killing ten and wounding eight in a movie theatre. The killer had simply said that he just felt like doing it. I couldn't believe what I was seeing or hearing! All those innocent lives taken for nothing!

Another report showed that immigrants being shot at while trying to cross the border to the U.S. Some of them were killed and others badly injured, including children! How can these people be so inhumane and merciless? Shot them down just because they had issues with foreigners living in this country? The next report showed how women who stood up for themselves in Iran were tortured. These were mothers and daughters who simply gave their honest opinion on how they wanted changes to take place in their country. They were women who believed that they have rights and want to express how they feel. They wanted their voices to be heard. No longer did they want to tolerate being treated unequal.

I decided to change the channel to Oprah's Soulful Sundays, just to get my mind riding on something peaceful rather than sad. The pains of the world were beginning to be just too much. Looking at sad faces and having sympathy for others seemed to be the norm these days. One of the guests on the show happened to be speaking about how we are surrounded by energy and that we are all made from this energy. The man also shared his belief that whether our thoughts are negative, or positive, they affect our world in a big way. Racism has ruined our country. There wasn't a place on planet Earth that could show that there were no disturbances between races or religion. The overwhelmingly ill thoughts of some people have corrupted our planet. Too many people have become immune to each other's feelings. Our society had changed for the worst in many ways.

TIME TO GET AWAY

The next day I headed to LAX to catch a 1:15 PM flight to Baltimore, MD. A dear friend of mine was celebrating another year and I wanted to be there for the occasion. As the plane took off, I noticed a gigantic rainbow in the sky. I didn't think too much of it, other than the fact that it was the biggest I had ever seen. My thoughts then drifted to how fortunate I was to have so many dear friends, near and far. It also crossed my mind how much faith we give the pilots as we soared higher and higher in the sky.

I enjoyed my flight and I always appreciate it when I get the chance to sit next to someone nice, knowledgeable or funny, especially when the feeling is mutual. Just as I had hoped, on this flight I sat next to a nice man whose complexion, hair, and smile reminded me of my Dad. He even had a scent that was surprisingly familiar and somehow made me feel safe.

I found out later that he retired early from Amtrak. He told me stories about his work and I shared the fond memories that I had when my father worked as a Red Cap at Santa

Fe. I also explained to him how much I loved the East Coast and that I had lots of family and friends there. Living in Washington, DC was nice back in the eighties. I have always felt that no person should ever live and die where they were born without experiencing the many differences in our United States. I've always had an interest to live bi-coastal and I still have plans to make it happen one day. I've thought many times of living abroad; to relocate for even six months would be an unforgettable experience, I'm sure.

After we exchanged names, Don, whom I like to call Mr. Porter, expressed that he's headed to Baltimore to attend a funeral. His news almost made me feel guilty that I was going to a party to have a good time, but then it hit me… everyone's day is numbered and we're all on borrowed time. Mr. Porter didn't appear sad at all; more like he had begun to accept the loss of his beloved sister. She was killed in a violent circumstance. He explained how she didn't take anything from anybody. He said, "Mari Porter was one fearless lady. She didn't care who she had to face. King Kong could be standing across from her and she wouldn't budge." He pulled out a picture from his wallet and showed me a family photo that included his brothers, Ryan and Sean, and his sister, Mari Porter. They all had richly dark complexions, which made their skin look velvety smooth. They were all quite attractive with perfect features, including high cheekbones, thick and perfectly shaped eye-brows, not to mention their full lips...especially Mari's. She had those lips that Hollywood folks are paying to get today, but it was obvious that the natural plumpness she had could only be God given.

Mr. Porter went on to tell me that Mari was a good soul. However, she was quite aggressive, even more so than any of her brothers. She excelled in sports and was one of the fastest on the track team. Everyone knew that once the baton was handed off to her, there was no stopping her. She had long legs, but didn't have the typical slender look like most track athletes. She had some meat on her bones. She wasn't exactly slim, but not at all overweight. She had a healthy and sexy look that was comparable to Serena Williams. Nevertheless, Mari was undisputed, one of the quickest out there...a true track star!

One December night, Mari and her girlfriends decided to grab a bite at a fast food restaurant. While they were there, a few folks in their age group came in and handed out flyers to attend a party nearby. The girls looked the information over and thought to take a chance on going. They weren't real familiar with the area, but felt they shouldn't have anything to worry about, especially since it was six of them.

Mari's girlfriends weren't as aggressive as she was, but they were no pushovers either. A few of them had parents who were former members of The Black Panthers or were advocates for other strong Black organizations. All of them had witnessed many confrontations about racism early in life. It was everyday conversation in their households.

When Mary and her girlfriends arrived at the party, they were happy to see people around their same age, which was early to mid-thirties. They were all good dancers and like at parties today, if a song they liked was played, they would just start dancing together. Those days of waiting for a guy to ask a girl to dance have long been over.

They all enjoyed themselves for a good hour or two, and then decided to get ready to head home. The party was just about to end as the DJ called out, 'last dance." Mari reached to get her jacket from the coat closet, but someone grabbed it at the same time. She pulled it toward her and the other person yanked it back. There was a real tug o' war going on! The next thing that happened shocked everyone there. Mari was stabbed and instantly fell to

the ground. A crowd of people surrounded her, including her girlfriends.

One of them yelled, "Call an ambu-
lance!" Hurry up! Please... Hurry!!!!"

Unfortunately, Mari didn't make
it. She had lost a lot of blood too
quickly. The person who stabbed her,
a girl by the name of Carla Huber,
tried to flee the scene, but there were
too many witnesses. Too many an-
gered faces that she confronted as she
tried to run.

The outcome was awfully sad. Unfortunately, the dramatic end resulted in more violence, arguments and
blaming each other, which in no time
became racial.

Carla feared for her life. She knew
that if she and Mari had punched it
out one-on-one, she would be the one
pushing up daisies, not Mari.

I thought once more that, "Something's got to give!"

Carla ended up doing time, but that wasn't enough for Mari's girls or her family. Her girlfriends never forgave Carla and wanted to somehow make her suffer. Now that she was out of jail, Carla thought that she had served her time and that everything should be forgotten, or at least that she shouldn't be receiving any heat from anyone. But, not to Mari's crew. Mari was the favorite in their clique and this girl, Carla, took her out. They felt robbed and so did Mari's family members. They loved Mari. She was the live wire at any gathering

Of course, Mr. Porter wasn't happy with what happened to his baby sister, but he accepted it. On the contrary, her younger brothers were just as furious as Mari's girlfriends. Ryan wanted something to pop off in honor of his baby sister. Sean just wanted Carla to pay, so he decided to start a movement focusing on Carla and her wrong doing. But not the typical peaceful movement, he felt that his sister's life had been literally taken away from them and he really wanted to create a violent movement. He wanted revenge! His goal was to get something started….it didn't matter what it was, just make sure it was racial!

As our plane landed, I told Mr. Porter what a pleasure it was to meet him and gave him my sincere condolences for his loss. He thanked me and assured me that everything will turn out fine. It was nice that he had such a positive attitude during such a trying time.

MADE IT HOME!

After a three-day weekend of fun festivities, I was back on the West Coast. My flight landed in Los Angeles extremely late due to two delays, so I decided to take off work the next day. Plus, I wasn't feeling all that good anyway.

I did leave the house to run a quick errand. There again, I noticed a rainbow. I was more amazed at this one because the colors looked different than any other rainbow. Also, it appeared to be closer than usual. It was quite striking.

As I headed home, I stopped to get a salad at my usual spot near the airport, and noticed Ashaki working outside. He usually works as a cashier, but on this afternoon he was in the parking lot sweeping up some of the early morning debris.

I got out of my car and said, "Hi Ashaki!"

He looked at me with the biggest grin and said "Heey Laa-dee," raising his broom up high.

I could see the excitement in Ashaki's eyes when he saw me. From the time that we met, I felt that we were both thankful that our paths had crossed. He was a new employee at Eaton's Salads and he was from Nigeria. He had beautiful skin and a perfectly shaped round, bald, head.

I remember when I first met him and how happy he seemed that I stopped to talk with him. He is a humble guy who wears a smile, but it is as if he is hiding his feelings. I felt that there was no doubt some pain in his heart, but I just didn't know exactly what or why.

Ashaki has lived in the states for only about two years, so he still had a very heavy African accent; enough to cause one to totally misunderstand his words. I asked him what made him decide to move to California and I received an answer that I was not expecting to hear, and one that caused a tug on my heart. What I learned was that Ashaki moved here to save his life! He went on to explain that the infamous group of folks in Nigeria, known as Boko Haram, caused him to flee.

Boko Haram is an aggresive Islamic extremist group based in northeastern Nigeria. I've heard that they have killed more people than any other terrorist group in the world. Ashaki says that they are the people who killed his beloved brother for simply for not joining them. They badly wanted his brother to join, but Ashaki said he was a Christian and that his family values would never lead him or his brother to join such a gruesome organization. I saw the pain in his eyes and felt it in my heart as he told me his story.

"Something's got to give," I thought. "Something has got to give!"

The lives of innocent people were taken for granted way too much, and with no remorse whatsoever. Ashaki expressed how much he missed his family. He left his parents and siblings, along with other relatives in Nigeria, and unfortunately, they were all still in hiding. His dream was to get his Green Card, so he would be able to move his family here, all twelve of them.

I have always had compassion for those who didn't get the opportunity of growing up with their parents (and siblings), especially in an enjoyable environment. And here, this guy had to flee to a faraway country, leaving his wife, kids, parents and all because of other people's stinking thinking. He had a very lucrative computer business

71

that he also had to leave behind. How unfortunate!

Growing up in a family setting teaches us so much, especially the little things like sharing and caring for others. Even when there are challenges and disagreements, most of us love our family regardless, and it is human nature to do so. We build so much from our family, as they are the very first people we share our innermost feelings with and whom we trust. I could not imagine having to be forced away from my loved ones.

WEEKEND TIME

Saturday morning, I got out of bed, gave thanks and thought that it would be a good day to hit the pool. It was hot and sunny, just shy of a hundred degrees, with no sign of a breeze in the forecast. I contemplated back and forth because I had just got a new hairdo, but gave in because of the heat.

Unbeknownst to me, there was a very nice Armenian family in the pool. They were my neighbors who lived somewhere in the complex, but I didn't know exactly where. We had met several times before in passing, while walking our dog, or at the mailbox. Suhana Avakian, her sister Lydia Kazarian, and their children, were enjoying the coolness of the water. The kids were having a grand time, playing Marco Polo and flipping upside down on their floaters. Lydia was kicking back, enjoying her hookah. I had seen a hookah pipe before, but never got the real reason behind it. She explained that puffing on a hookah is not only relaxing, but your taste buds get to dance in all the different tobacco flavors. The vapors smelled delicious as she was burning the flavor of watermelon. I took a toke or two, but it didn't interest me. It seems to be quite popular though with the younger generation.

Suhana is a wonderful person and always has a kind word. Her inner beauty compliments her outer beauty because she is as pretty as she is kind. It is her nature to please those around her. Without much notice, Suhana disappeared from the pool area for a good thirty minutes or so. I had begun to bask in the sun, hoping to get just a tad bit more chocolate. I rubbed down with some coconut oil and shea butter, then kicked back with my eyes closed, in total relaxation.

Soon after, I happened to look up and there was Suhana at the gated pool entrance with a large tray filled with chips and salsa, appetizers, and, of course, Coronas. She offered me a beer and I obliged – it was quite tasty

and delightfully quenched my thirst. I
told Shuana how nice it was of her to
bring the refreshments for all of us to
enjoy. We both swam up to the edge of
the pool and began to touch on how
easy it is to be nice and how much it is
needed with all the chaos in the world
today. We agreed on how effortless it
is to be kind and respectful of others,
while being the opposite takes so much
effort...much more than we realize.

As we continued to talk, I sensed
that she had something she wanted to
get off her chest and that this was the
perfect opportunity to do it. I could
tell that she felt safe with me, therefore,
she trusted me. She wanted to fill me
in on something that had been haunt-
ing her. Suhana began to explain how
bad things are in her country of Iran.
Moreover, she mentioned how awful it

was in terms of religious wars, and that they were ongoing, and have been for centuries. She mentioned the astronomical number of people who died there daily. It was hard to imagine.

Remembering from a little girl, Suhana told how the sights and sounds of war were forever etched in her mind. Tears came to her eyes as she spoke about all the young and innocent children in the Middle East who were killed without knowing why. They didn't understand the concept of a religious war, and even if they did, they couldn't do anything about it. It was sad to learn that people she knew all her life had turned against her because of religious differences. The Muslims and Christians are at war and it has become normal, everyday life. Living in her country was so dangerous and chaotic that just like Ashaki, she had to make a major life change.

She had to make an abrupt departure from Iran, which meant that she had to leave expensive properties behind. She literally had to walk away from her investments. She sadly explained how much she and her husband would like to go back to sell their properties, but the risk of being killed was simply just too high. People who have known her from a little girl would have no problem to look her in the eyes and then kill her because of her religion. This gave both of us a sinking feeling in the gut. We both thought, again, about how terrible and unfortunate it is to have so much hatred in the world.

I immediately thought of the words that I'm beginning to say more and more these days, "Something's got to give."

MORE OF THE SAME

The next morning, I clicked the remote back to CNN and the breaking news read:

> Black teen shot and killed –
> water gun mistaken for real gun
> Two women raped at school
> dance – left drugged and un-
> conscious
> Ten killed at movie theatre

Four White students beat up at
school for being gay
ISIS attacks, 122 people dead
and counting
Ku Klux Klan sightings in Whit-
tier
And on and on...

Each day there was more dreadful
news from around the globe, and the
reports became increasingly disturb-
ing. Regrettably, stories like this had
become the norm in our society. It was
as if we were going back in time, taking two steps forward and more than
two back.

"Something has got to give!" I
thought again.

STRANGE DAY

Two days later....

Another fresh morning and when I arose, I realized that in spite of all the chaos, we are still blessed because so many people around the world didn't wake up this morning. Sadly, people are heart-broken because of the ugly, selfish acts of others;

acts that have caused untimely deaths of their loved ones.

I remembered that this is the day the members of our community, both young and old, had planned to meet in hopes to find ways to bring everyone together. All were welcomed. The plan was to come together in an informal manner to discuss some of the negative issues related to hatred and racism, which was growing rampant within races all over the globe. Every human being deserves respect. People needed to brainstorm on ideas to put in place to treat each other better. They wanted answers and felt that it is everyone's responsibility to get involved.

Community leaders had agreed that they selected the perfect location for this gathering, realizing that the location offered wide-open outdoor space. It held lots of people, plus right next to it was a large park. This left a massive, open area, which gave plenty of room for people to meet. A good-sized facility room was also available for our use and included a few large flat screen televisions.

After I got dressed, I grabbed my purse and keys then headed to the area where we were all to meet. I had envisioned a large area, but as I was looking for a place to park, the area seemed much bigger than I had imagined. When I arrived, I parked my car and anxiously hopped out. I was looking forward to being involved in a positive movement to help heal our world. I loved the fact that this project was starting within my own community, and I couldn't wait to see how many of my family and neighbors would show up.

As I hit the button to lock my car, I glanced to my right and could not believe who and what I saw!! There was Chase *and* Malcolm, and each had a bunch of folks with them. I also saw Michael, holding hands with his girl, Corina, as they walked in front of their infamous entourage. As my eyes scanned the area, there was Ryan and Sean, walking within a few feet of the girls from Mari's crew, and they had hundreds of people behind them!

To my far left was Carla Huber and her friends, many of whom she met in jail. There were various gangs there too. Most people looked as if they came to accomplish something because expressions on their faces were serious, demanding, and hard. I honestly felt

that something bad was going to happen because no one looked like they
were here to talk to about unity, but
God knows, we needed to. They all
seemed concerned, but unfriendly,
some even mad.

As I maneuvered through the
crowd, I saw NAACP members, KKK,
Black Panthers, and other well-orga-
nized organizations. There was a mix-
ture of all kinds of folks. Although the
turnout was quite unexpected, it was
great to see so many people show up,
nonetheless.

I think that deep down some people wanted to start chaos, while the
others wanted to end it. The more I
walked through the crowd, I saw some
people that I knew or that looked familiar, to say the least. Later, I observed
that some people were engaged in

conversation, seemingly debating over racism and other negative topics. A few folks huddled with friends, however, the majority looked to be surprised and uncertain. People began shouting louder and louder and it became more difficult to hear each other.

Mr. Bomar, the City Mayor, tapped on his microphone and said, 'Excuse me, ladies and gentlemen, may I have your attention, please?! Please, may I have your attention?!"

As the crowd quieted down, Mr. Bomar went on to tell everyone how much he appreciated the huge attendance. He then tried to bring the meeting to some type of order, but it was too late. The area had quickly overfilled. The crowd now spilled over to the sidewalks and into the streets.

Suddenly, the loudest boom imaginable sounded off! It was like the sound of lightning in the South, magnified a thousand times. It was almost too loud to bear. The day became darker and eerie. For a moment, I had to think whether it was night or early morning because I had quickly lost track.

I noticed that the leaves had begun to softly tumble across the ground and flutter in the trees. Then the winds increasingly ramped up, minute by the minute. Shortly thereafter, the winds started to howl at unusually high speeds and the trees were now swishing and swaying. It was magnificent and scary at the same time.

Although people were there collectively, there was a feeling of being alone. But, through the loud speaker people heard the words, "Be calm."

"Don't panic. Everything is going to be okay." Some people became frightened, causing some family and friends to hug each other and hold hands.

Next, we saw "CNN – Stay tuned for breaking news" appear across the large monitor. A few seconds later, the news correspondents were in awe! They had noticed the same darkness, swirling sounds, strong winds and frantic looks that were on everyone's faces. It was bad enough to witness all this strangeness happening in my small community, but then to find out that this bizarre scenario was taking place worldwide, was hard to grasp! Fear began to be the predominant look on everyone's face, even those who pretended to be so cool, fearless, and strong, because they, too, were afraid!

The winds blew so strong that it tore people apart and had them bumping into each other. Folks were looking for their family members, friends, or someone they could recognize, but to no avail. There was a sweeping warmth of air, as if a gigantic fan had been turned on, but backwards. The air was pulling in, not blowing out! What a weird sensation it was.

Then the darkness deepened, almost blinding us from each other. The trees swayed, the petals blew from the flowers, the leaves frantically danced in the wind. Next, a light, fine, powdery dust filled the air causing us to have no more sight of one another than a squinting possibility.

The wind began to whistle, but backwards! People were speechless, trying to look to the sky for answers, but the disturbance of the dust made it impossible! Many were screaming at the top of their lungs because the conditions were so erratic.

Gradually, the darkness began to lighten and the sky turned into various colors of soft hues in red, green, yellow and blue. It appeared to be a gigantic rainbow! This was something that no one had ever experienced before. As this odd inhale of wind became louder, the dusty swirls in the air became more intense. People could not believe what they saw or how they felt. The confusion and wonderment was beyond comprehension.

WHAT WAS IT?

During the chaos, there was a loud noise that seemed to echo throughout the world. At first, it was just the sound of chaotic winds. However, as people listened more intently, the winds began to give the exact sound of the beginning of a sneeze. In fact, no one doubted that it was a sneeze, but that couldn't be...or could it? A sneeze? Coming from where? Yet, people heard, ah-ah-ah, ahhhhhhhh-hhhh. The inhale was so strong that it sucked everything from everybody!

Feeling as if being in an enormous vacuum, people felt a huge pull on their entire body as colors swirled around and seemingly through them! The pull from the wind was so strong that people were actually lifted several inches off the ground! Each time they heard ah-ah-ahh, they felt another sensational pull that was sensed throughout their entire body making their skin feel odd and tingle all over. By now, everyone had their eyes closed for three reasons: 1) They were so afraid; 2) The wind was so fierce, it tightly pulled their eyes; and 3) All the dust! They had no choice but to close them and keep them closed!

People were lifted in the air with the strongest gust ever known to man, and out of nowhere came the exhale, Chuuuuuuuuuuuuuuuuuuuuuu! The winds were reaching over three hundred miles per hour now and more dust and whirls were in the air, making the colors more vivid. The screams were deafening and the confusion beyond chaotic.

When the trees lashed back and forth this time, they went in the opposite direction! Trees bent every which a way, but they never broke. Suddenly, just like the wind and dust started, the swaying of the trees came to a subtle stop. As the winds died down people tumbled over each other as they were brought back down to their feet. Amazingly, not one person was hurt. You could hear murmurings of everyone about what had just happened. But, what had happened? What was the cause of all of this and how could they possibly still be alive? People felt different, but just as important, they looked different. Something amazing had happened and it had everyone in wonder.

WHO ARE WE?

Well, no one could have ever imagined it, but the rainbow sneezed! That big 'ole rainbow gave the strongest inhale and exhale possible. When it did, lives changed forever. You see, the rainbow was entirely fed up with the way people were treating each other. It became upset and knew that it had the power to make a change in the world, even it was by force.

It could no longer take the racism and critical destruction taking place globally, seeing so many people hurt and suffering. Too many people were in pain and for way too long. Many lives were taken which meant that an excessive amount of hearts were broken. From the elderly to babies, people were living terribly, and it didn't stop there.

Man's evil ways even spilled over to the mistreatment of animals and plants, which caused horrible pollution to our dear planet Earth. Our world became plagued with severe weather changes, ranging from tsunamis to huge widespread fires. Some areas experienced droughts, hurricanes and tornadoes – all so devastating!

The earthquakes mirrored broken hearts, representing the heavy heartaches of our planet. There was no consciousness in hurting one another, taking from each other, or even worse, killing one another. Racism had reached the top. It was over the top! There were too many innocent people being destroyed simply because of the color of their skin or religion. The rainbow felt that all the love and beauty in the world was being ignored, trampled on and literally rejected. This was all quite painful and disappointing to the rainbow. It knew the radiance *of* the world because it gave radiance *to* the world.

When people could finally open their eyes, the first thing they noticed was that their skin color had changed. Not only that, their hair and features changed along with it. What took place reminded me of something you might see in the Outer Limits or a scientific movie. The funny thing is that when people talked, some of them had their native voice, while others didn't – this confused them even more. It was strange.

Now people were totally mystified because they were no longer sure of who was who....who belonged to what nationality, what race?

They were forced to think before they act because their thoughts were, "Now, if I hurt this person, whom I think is White, he may really be my brother, of African descent."

I could be hurting my own mother or child for crying out loud. Or, if I want to do wrong to this Asian person, he might be related to me, because now I am not sure of who I am!

The rainbow's sneeze mixed us all up. I was Black, but now I'm White! I was White, but now I'm Indian! I was Mexican, but now I'm Cuban! I was Ethiopian, but now I'm Polish! And so on. And the features... Everyone's features changed, some slightly and others more drastic. It was mind boggling to say the least. People were now afraid to harm anyone simply because they never knew for sure what race was before them – and no one wanted to mistreat their own kind.

The phenomenon was worldwide. This change affected everyone's mind. They had no choice, really. People finally began to act like they had good sense and morals.

"Please," "Thank you," and "Excuse me," became everyday language again.

People offered common courtesy to anyone who walked in their path. It was a pleasure to help someone if you could. In fact, folks went out of their way to help others because when they looked at them, they saw their own family members – friends too, but mostly their immediate family. Some even saw their ancestral traits, which were so powerful that it made many of them cry joyous tears! It was a beautiful sight to see. People were hugging each other tight. Then they'd stop and look at each other with tears flowing, smile and go on to the next person and hug them. It was obvious to everyone that we were all one.

Words like "homelessness" finally disappeared because those who had housing, lovingly offered to share their space with others who didn't have shelter. Everyone now slept in a warm bed. Starvation became a thing of the past because people were happy to share their food with others. There was no such thing as rape, child abuse or murder. The exquisite differences we had were divvyed up and shared with all of humankind. People experienced and explored the different cultural traditions, rituals and recipes, and enjoyed every minute of it.

Some people felt strong instincts as they prepared dishes from their previous nationality. They also took joy in learning how other nationalities prepared their food. Many were amazed that they could they do it so well. Some found it stereotypical. For example, one man who was previously Indian had never tasted collard greens, was now Black and prepared a perfect soul food meal. He was startled that he knew how to prepare it so well, as he didn't remember growing up eating

fried chicken, greens or cornbread...
let alone cook it!

The different traditions and rituals really had folks astounded! People
who were previously African or Puerto
Rican were now doing Asian dances.
Folks who were now Canadian beautifully sewed Indian clothes. It seemed
odd, yet it felt right! Everyone now
had a new lease on life, whether they
wanted to or not. Their lives were refreshed and renewed. Negativity of the
past had been erased. Love resonated
throughout our entire world, and it
solved all life's problems.

So many companies went out of
business since their services were no
longer necessary. Companies that sold
door locks, car alarms, guns, burglar
alarms for the home, and other devic-
es for protection of thievery were all

out of business. Jobs like policemen and security guards became obsolete. Jails were no longer needed simply because crime no longer existed. People were now honest and would never think of doing such a thing as taking something that wasn't theirs. Everyone left doors and windows unlocked. In fact, on those hot summer nights, they left them open overnight and not once did anyone ever have a problem. The rainbow took care of all that madness.

Our environment had also changed. There was no such thing as a drought or flooding. People began taking care of Mother Earth like they loved her, and appreciated all her beauty for a change. The flowers and trees grew and blossomed so beautifully, filling the planet with lovely mixtures of fragrances. All animals were loved and treated as family members. People had dominion over animals like they always had, but now they were all loved as if they were their children. They were never chained up or locked down, taught to fight, or suffered in any kind of way. The animals lived happily and received a lot of attention. They were no longer abused.

The world was such a beautiful place. Anger, hate, disrespect, dishonesty and racism, had been replaced with love, respect, integrity, honesty and peace. People had finally concluded that when the rainbow sneezed, it changed the world in a dramatic way.

It was all to the good for the good. Something finally gave!

AFTER THE DUST SETTLED

Van Miller, a kid who was very interested in science, was extremely intrigued when the rainbow sneezed. On that extraordinary day, amid the strange winds, remarkable changes, and dust in the air, he managed to capture some dust from the rainbow and trap it in a jar. Once he felt that he had a substantial amount, he quickly put the top on the jar and screwed it on tight. Van later taped the top to the jar to make sure it was secure, put it in a box, and tucked it away in his garage. He wanted to make sure that it was out of the way from everyone because deep down, he knew that he had something extraordinary.

One year later....

In preparation for her event, Van's mother Lucille Johnston, asked him to help clean out the garage because she was planning a huge sale. Lucille was known for having the best garage sales. Everyone knew that she would offer the best prices ever! She was a shopaholic and had countless items, many of which would still have its original price tag.

It was her therapy to find deals, even on items she didn't or couldn't use. It was just the idea of getting a bargain that drove her to shop. Van had a love-hate relationship when it came to her garage sales because he hated doing the work, but loved the fact that his mom was going to pay him for his help. Another thing he liked was that he would always re-discover a few of his old video games or tennis shoes that were once his favorites.

After working in the garage for a couple of hours, Van's task was just about complete. As he moved the last few boxes around, he glanced over to the corner and could not believe what was in view...the box holding the jar of dust! It had been a whole year since he put the box there, so he was completely surprised when he saw it. His mind drifted for a moment, remembering how incredible that day was and the moment he captured the dust. He reflected on how noisy and crowded that day was, and how life changing it was as well.

When he finished cleaning out the garage, Van gave a quick shout out to his mom that he was going to Winston Jansen's house, who was his best friend. He quickly picked up the box, put it in his backpack and hopped on his bike. Van rode his bike over to Winston's house and told him all about what was in the jar. He wasn't sure if the dust had vanished or if it was still in the jar, and he was more than curious to find out. Winston excitedly remembered the day the rainbow sneezed and thought that Van could be holding a fortune. If the dust was still in the jar, he believed that Van held particles of the most important day in our history. He suggested that Van give the box to James David to see if he could make any sense of whatever was in there.

James David (aka Professor David) was a well-known biochemist and scientist, and like everyone else, he was still puzzled about the unique rainbow experience. Therefore, he welcomed the idea to be called upon to decipher the special dust, however, he couldn't offer any guarantee as to what he'd find, if anything at all.

The next morning, Professor David arrived at his lab quite early, as he was just as excited as Van was about the dust. This was clearly a project with an uncertain outcome because up until now, there was no such thing

as dust from a rainbow. He anxiously walked over to the table where the
jar sat, opened it up and began to re-
move some of the particles and placed
them on a clear piece of glass. He then
turned up the lights as bright as they
could go because he wanted to be sure
to see everything, and miss nothing.
At first when he observed the particles,
all he could see was a variety of colors
all meshed together in a humongous
blob. When he looked closer, it appeared as if there were hundreds, if not
thousands, of patterns in three shapes -
rounded, pointed, and straight.

To get a clearer picture, Professor
David had to use a special eyepiece,
one that he uses for only his intricate
tasks, such as this one. He unlocked the
cabinet and carefully removed the very
expensive eyepiece, and placed it in its

holder. He quickly walked back to the lab table and when he glanced down this time, he could see the objects a bit clearer, but he still couldn't make out what they were. The challenge was that the pieces were sticking together.

He grabbed his finest tweezers and carefully began to probe and prod, trying to pull the pieces apart. As he moved the pieces around, he saw the most beautiful sight ever. Hearts! They were beautifully shaped hearts!! Now it made sense why he originally saw the various shapes; it depended on what part of the heart was in view. The Professor smiled as he happily lined up the hearts on a piece of glass for further observation. He didn't think it could be possible, but the hearts seemed to lovingly smile back at him.

So, it was hearts! Loving hearts were sneezed across the world, in every color that existed. Each heart had a true purpose and knew exactly where to go. The hearts were happy to do what they were supposed to do and that was to spread love. It worked because ever since the rainbow sneezed, people dealt with each other heart to heart. We realized that what really mattered was what was inside one's heart and that we are all here to spread love.

The tiny hearts were then placed in a second device that had a higher magnification. Professor David felt fortunate to decipher the hearts and could hardly wait to break the news. This task was by far, his most cherished accomplishment. He took a moment to relish in his newest discovery. Letting his thoughts percolate, he brewed up a cup of coffee and briefly read through some of his mail. He really loved being at the lab working on various projects, as it was his official think tank. Now that the task was completed, the Professor picked up the phone and decided to call his wife, Vivian, to let her know that he would be heading home shortly.

Vivian David was extremely proud of her husband and whenever he made a major discovery she would feel so honored to be his wife. On the other hand, the Professor believed he owed much of his success to her. Back when he was in college, Vivian sacrificed a lot of her own personal desires so that he could fulfill his. She was a screenwriter and was quite good at it. In fact, of her seven screenplays, four of them made it to Broadway. She was always surprised that her work became such big hits because that was not why she wrote.

Vivian was inspired to write ever since she was a kid because she never believed in fairytales or make believe. At an early age, she realized that someone made up the stories about the tooth fairy, Santa Claus, the Easter Bunny, etc., and she wanted to write her own.

Vivian eventually put her creative juices aside and realized that it was more important to devote her time to her family. She was a stay-at-home mom and enjoyed raising their three sons. It became apparent that she loved raising them much more than her writing. All three of the boys were very successful; one owned several franchised Holistic Healing Centers, one was a famous chef, and the other was an extremely talented musician. They all had different lifestyles, but made it a point to have family time, even if was just to fly in town for dinner or go to a football game together.

THE CODES

Just as he started to dial Vivian's number, the magnifying device gave a loud, continuous beep, so Professor David hung up the phone, and immediately went to check on the hearts. While he knew that discovering the hearts was a spectacular accomplishment, after he checked the final lab results, he had to sit down and take deep breaths because he was stunned. The final lab results had him speechless.

The results showed that the code for human lifespan was imprinted on the hearts, meaning that people could find out how long one would live. Just like the hearts, never in history has anything like this ever been considered. Discovering the hearts was one thing, but the codes found within the hearts had him scratching his head.

The professor realized that the impact of the tiny codes could be devastating. He knew that such news would have some people excited, some petrified, and those who would refuse to hear anything more about it. The brave and curious might want to know their date of departure, and possibly look forward to obtaining such information.

Exposing the date of one's expira-
tion made people realize how much
they love and need each other, even
more so. For some, only a few life expe-
riences were left, while others still had
many to come before them. Having
the ability to know one's end of life was
certainly something to think about. It
was one of those things that you either
want to know or don't want to know,
especially if one's time was coming up
sooner rather than later.

Putting this all together, Professor
David set it up, for those who wanted to know, and made it possible
to make an appointment at any of
the Heart Health Centers. All that
was required was to schedule a MRI
and request your date. Some were
relieved when they received their
date, while others felt ill from just
the thought of the short time they

had left. Ironically, some people were ready to go. They had love ones they wanted to meet up with, but for the most part, people wanted to stay here on Earth for as long as possible.

One lady's reading was seven months. Another was two years. While another one read fifteen years, and so on, up to the hundreds. People began to gather amongst each other to see who had what date, as if they were at school gathered around to see who passed their finals.

A man who had twenty-two years remaining wanted to accomplish all his items on his bucket list. He had reached his goal of some, but realized there were others left undone. He believed that he had a good chance of checking off everything on his list. An older woman was given fifteen more

119

years and felt very lucky since she had already been around for over seventy-six years now.

For the most part, the majority still had many years to live. Some of the people who received shorter amounts of time felt the sting of it. Some were very ill and had been for a long time. Others hadn't been sick a day in their life. This really put perspective on things. Life expectancy is something that we hardly ever think about, especially when we're young. Older individuals may think about it now and then, but I think most people contemplate about life more than they do death.

As people received their date, some jumped with joy while others were obviously and understandably in tears. Some felt fortunate while others felt they were cheated. One thing that became clear to everyone was that everybody needed somebody. People understood that it was impossible for man to complete any task without the help of others....that no man or woman became great on their own. Subconsciously, we may have felt the need of others, but now consciously, we recognized it. People paid attention to the fact that there was a race against time for them that connected to others.

People realized that there was no guarantee about anything. There were mentors, doctors, professors, artists and gurus that had relevant information to give to others so that they could succeed. None of us know of *all* the connections required to complete one's mission. There were reasons that people connected with some people and not others. What we do know is that we need each other.

━━┥┝━━

What if you knew your code and fell into one of these categories?

One…
You want to be a musician and you take lessons. You're talented, and you find out that you have fifty-five more years to live. You meet the top producer in the business, whose style you love, and techniques you want to learn, but she has only three months left to live. You need her, and have a short time to gather everything you need from her that will enhance *your* project before *she* exits the earth.

Two…
You are a responsible young lady and are ready for marriage and children. You happily find out that you have seventy years left. You've realized that you are in love with a young man whom you want to marry and be the father of your children. You both find out that he has only three years left of life. Do you proceed spending as much time as possible together knowing his departure will be much earlier than yours, or do you seek another mate with a longer lifespan?

Or three…
You now know that certain members of your family have very short lifespans. They make an extra effort to spend time with you, because you might be needed so that they can reach their personal goals. Do you make yourself

extra available to spend quality time with them?

What would you do if you knew? Would you love more? Should you love more anyway?

"Whether we are referring to a family member, friend, co-worker, stranger, or enemy, it is necessary to recognize each human being with love because we never know who is required to help us move forward. We never know who will connect us to the next important person, place or thing necessary to complete our journey."

Once and for all, we all get it! Mother Earth, everyone and everything on the planet has gone through so many years of suffering. But we are all on the same page now, for we are all one. People began to realize that all of us are important and that we need each other for every single task in the world. They remembered that they could not create anything on their own.

The light bulb finally came on to the realization of knowing that the food they ate, the clothes they wore, the chair they sat in, the lotion rubbed on their skin, the jewelry they wore, the shampoo they used, the pen they write with, the car they drove, the ear-phones they listed with, the shoes they wore, the glasses that allowed them to see, the coffee they drank, the ball they bounced, the pool they swam in, the instruments that made music, the umbrella to cover the rain, the candles that brought light, the coat to keep them warm, the soap to cleanse their body, the bed to sleep in, the computer I'm typing on... So on, and so on.

It was learned that every day from the moment we arise until the time we retire for the night, we have used other people's stuff, so to speak. We feed off each other. When people learn something and master it, everyone gets to benefit from it.

The more we realize this truth, the easier it will be for us to appreciate people of all races. Everybody contributes. Additionally, we'll have a better understanding of how valuable we all are together. What a difference a day makes, an hour, a minute, a second – the understanding of love and appreciation has transformed everyone and is welcomed by all. People are going to and fro, making things happen when they can as best as they can, without harming anyone! It is in our nature to grow and expand our opportunities – to live better, reach higher do more for ourselves, as well as others.

A NEW DAY

Still amazed at all the changes in the world, I got up, gave thanks, and headed out to work. It was a Friday, the day before the 4th of July holiday. When I got to the office everyone was in a good mood, as usual. Every single person in the office was kind and considerate. It was so nice to see such a beautiful blend of all the races, finally together as one. Life was so nice that even the birds seemed to chirp more and louder than before. It seemed like people were overly polite, but they had been so far from it for so long that they weren't over doing it all. Life became greater, grander and more glorious!

Several co-workers were planning go to Andy's Place for happy hour and asked if I wanted to go. I gave it a thought and decided, why not? I always head straight home after work, and it's time I start to venture out some. I had already been thinking that I need to get out more.

The group met at Andy's Place, an establishment that everyone liked, attracting both younger and older crowds. Everybody just blended in to-gether and had a good time. The hap-py hour menu was great – half off on

Margaritas and wine, and had a variety of finger foods for just two dollars. The dance floor was incredible since it had an extremely sophisticated lighting system that was soft, but had LED light sensors that highlighted the dance moves; kind of like the old school disco lights, but nowhere near as bold.

Even if you didn't dance, you'd have a good time because the regulars there were all excellent dancers, and they would always put on a show toward closing. We had a big table that comfortably seated ten and the location was perfect. Andy's Place was known for its Cadillac Margaritas so I thought I'd try one...or two. It was a fun night as we all took turns dancing and singing Karaoke. I think the more people drank, the braver they became. I was shocked to see that some of my coworkers could sing so well, but just as shocked to see those who really needed to just drop the mic. It was all in fun though, and we were all having such a great time.

As I got up to get a drink, a nice looking young man bumped into me and quickly said, "Pardon me."

I replied, "No problem."

I saw him again and this time he asked me if I wanted to dance, and there we were on the dance floor. He was a tall, nice-looking guy, brown skinned with beautiful hair. I couldn't really tell his nationality, but that didn't matter. He was quite smooth on the dance floor as he would kick one leg out to the side, slide it back in, then do a funky twist with his feet, reminding me of the Godfather of Soul, JB. I hadn't danced in a while, so I had to work at it a bit to stay on step and to keep up with him.

Later, I found out his name was Anthony Roberts. He had a nice beard and wore his hair medium length and care-free. His personality was calm and he wore a casual navy-blue suit with a white unbuttoned shirt, and red shoes and hat. His outfit appropriately honored the Independence Day holiday colors. His suit was made of pure linen and gave the wrinkles that only linen can give. He looked old-school cool, reminding me of back in the day.

After dancing through three or four songs, I brought Anthony over to our table and introduced him to my co-workers. He and I laughed, danced and talked the night away. I could tell that he was from good stock. A true gentleman! At the end of the night he asked me for my digits and I gave them to him without much hesitation.

The next day Anthony called me and asked me to lunch. We went to a Sushi restaurant only because he loved Sushi. I didn't particularly care for it, but I knew he did. To avoid suggesting a different restaurant, I simply ordered the California Rolls, the one item that I like, and it was good.

While the conservation was casual, I could tell that he liked me, a lot. I was trying to catch myself, however, I was beginning to like him too. He had a real easiness about him that was attractive, and there was absolutely no pressure which made me very comfortable. Just before we left, Anthony paid the bill and we headed to his car. As he walked me to the passenger side, he stopped just before he opened the door and gave me a stare. I was hoping that he'd stop, but he didn't. He kept staring for few seconds. Then he gently kissed me on my forehead and said, "There is something real special about you."

I replied with a "Thank you," and I told him, "Everyone is special. It's just that most of us don't know it."

Anthony smiled at me, shut the car door and walked around to his side. We enjoyed conversation on a lot of subjects. Everything about him felt right. He took me back to my job and told me that he'd talk to me later. I thanked him for the lunch and he went on his way. As the days and weeks went by, Anthony and I seemed to get closer and closer. Before we knew it, we developed a delightful friendship. I felt that whatever I was going through, he'd be right there to support me and if I'm not mistaken, the feeling was mutual. I had been longing to meet someone that I enjoyed spending my time with, especially for those weekend getaways and he fit perfect! I felt blessed to have Anthony in my life, he was so refreshing.

The next Friday evening, I called Anthony and asked him if he wanted to come by for dinner. The weather was on the cold side, so I decided to make homemade chili. Anthony (and everyone else) loves my chili. When he arrived, I greeted him with a big hug and kiss and handed him a glass of my special red wine. It was my last bottle of one of those unique wines from Trader Joe's. Every day is special these days, and I certainly thought

Anthony was special enough to share it with – in fact, it was my pleasure to do so.

It was obvious that we enjoyed each other's company and that our relationship was better than good. We had that spontaneity thing going on and I loved it. I also loved that he enjoyed filling me with surprises. He always surprised me with wonderful excursions. He was a spur-of-the-moment type of guy and loved to travel, just like me. He mentioned that he had to go to Washington for business and that if I wanted to go, he would add some personal time and we could enjoy the weekend together.

I replied with an excited "Yes!"

A week later, we were at Los Angeles airport in line at the security check point and we had a conversation about how polite people were. Very vaguely, we remembered how impatient folks used to be at airports, especially those who were running late. We noticed throughout our travels that everywhere we went, people were kind and respectful. The rainbow sneeze was so powerful and positive.

Just as Anthony finished up his business in Washington, he got a call from a buddy of his who was in town and wanted to get together. So, that evening Anthony and his friend, Brandon Stahl, and his date, Lisa Coleman, joined us at a jazz supper club.

The club sat up on a hill and we had such a great view of the city. Washington State is beautiful, filled with picturesque little cities, especially at night. The live entertainment was wonderful and the atmosphere was quite intimate. The size and ambience of the club reminded me of one of my favorite spots in Los Angeles, Catalina Bar and Grill. Brandon and Lisa both had charming personalities. The four of us had a lot in common. I mentioned to Lisa that I was writing a book and she quickly let me know that she was a publisher. I thought, perfect! I told her that I would be contacting her in the very near future, and she offered me a big discount since I knew Anthony. She stated that Brandon and Anthony have been friends for a very long time. We all had a great, relaxing, evening.

While we were waiting for our server to bring our check, an older mysteriously-looking gentleman came over to our table and asked Anthony if he could speak with him for just a few moments.

Anthony said, "Sure, no problem."

They stepped away from the table and walked over to the patio area to talk. A few moments later, Brandon excused himself and went to the men's room. Lisa and I refreshed our lipstick and exchanged phone numbers. We promised to keep in touch. In about five minutes, both Brandon and Anthony walked back to our table with a different look on their face than when they left. Once Anthony paid the bill, he quickly motioned to us ladies that it was time to go.

As we headed out, Brandon said, "I'll see you later, Chase."

I was startled because I didn't know whom he was referring to. Anthony made a gesture and they shook hands. Lisa, Brandon and I gave each other a farewell hug, then we all left the scene.

That night flowed so perfectly,
right up until the end because that's
when something seemed odd. As
we were walking to the car, I asked
Anthony what that older gentleman
wanted in the restaurant. And even
more curiously, why Brandon called
him Chase. He explained that Chase
was his first name and Anthony was
his middle name. He mentioned that
only his close friends call him by that
name, and that he and Brandon had
known each other for decades. His
explanation made reasonable sense,
but I still had a funny feeling in my
stomach that something peculiar was
happening.

In just that moment, Anthony's features seemed to remind me of someone, but I couldn't pin point who. His
red hat also became more noticeable

to me and brought up a vague memory of him...like a déjà vu was taking place. I knew in my spirit that I had met him before, but just couldn't put the pieces together – then it hit me! The red hat, scruffy beard, the style, the smooth talker!!

I said, "Chase! You're Chase!!!! Chase Roberts!!"

Even though his complexion was a different color, it was Chase.

"We've met before! Do you remember me? You know my cousin Malcolm!" I exclaimed.

Chase Anthony replied, "Well, this is embarrassing, because I don't quite remember you. Ever since the rainbow sneezed, my memory has changed somewhat. Some things I clearly remember, others are vague, and then there are things I don't remember at all, so please bear with me. Chase pulled me closer to him with a serious look on his face and said, "Not to change the subject, but I have something important to tell you."

"I don't think we're quite ready for the news that the man in the restaurant gave me. In fact, I don't think anyone is, but I've got to tell you!" I was beginning to feel a little sad because it hurt my feelings that he didn't remember me, although I understood why he didn't. Without hesitation, I nervously asked, "What did he tell you?" "What did that man tell you?"

Chase replied, "I don't know how you'll take this, but that man was a Prophet. He has been here before and he has lived many lives. The man was clairvoyant!" Chase went on to say,

"The entire time that the man spoke, I felt a light around us. I could feel my own aura become brighter and stronger. I felt warmth and love magnified." What a loving Soul he was!"

Chase asked, "Honey, are you ready for what I am about to tell you?

I replied, "Yes, please tell me. What did that man say?"

Chase says, "Well, he told me that the rainbow is going to cough soon!"

"Cough? Did he actually say cough?" I asked.

Chase replied with an emphatic "YES!"

A few moments later, that struck both of us so funny that we laughed and laughed, until we could hardly catch our breath. Eventually, we fell asleep in each other's arms. The next morning when I opened my eyes, I peeked out the window and noticed a soft rainbow forming slowly across the sky. Then I realized that this was all a dream.

The End ☺

FAMOUS QUOTES ON RACISM AND DIVERSITY

"Hating people because of their color is wrong. And it doesn't matter which color does the hating. It's just plain wrong." – Muhammad Ali

"Our true nationality is mankind." – H.G. Wells

"We've got to face the fact that some people say you fight fire best with fire, but we say you put fire out best with water. We say you don't fight racism with racism. We're gonna fight racism with solidarity." – Fred Hampton

"We can move in that direction as a country, in greater polarization – black people amongst blacks, and white amongst whites, filled with hatred toward one another. Or we can make an effort, as Martin Luther King did, to understand and to comprehend, and replace that violence, that stain of bloodshed that has spread across our land, with an effort to understand, compassion and love...What we need in the United States is not division; what we need in the United

States is not hatred; what we need in the United States is not violence and lawlessness, but is love and wisdom, and compassion toward one another, and a feeling of justice toward those who still suffer within our country, whether they be white or whether they be black." – Robert F. Kennedy

"You can't hate the roots of a tree and not hate the tree." – Malcolm X

"Every miserable fool who has nothing at all of which he can be proud, adopts as a last resource pride in the nation to which he belongs; he is ready and happy to defend all its faults and follies tooth and nail, thus reimbursing himself for his own inferiority." – Arthur Schopenhauer

"Until the philosophy of which hold one race superior and another inferior is finally and permanently discredited and abandoned...Everything is war. Me say war. That is until there is no longer 1st class and 2nd class citizens of any nation...Until the color of a man's skin is of no more significance than the color of his eyes, me say war. That until the basic human rights are equally guaranteed to all without regard to race, me say war!" - Haile Selassie

"Men build too many walls and not enough bridges." – Joseph Fort Newton

"The piano keys are black and white but they sound like a million colors in your mind." – Maria Cristina Mena

"Ignorance and prejudice are the hand-maidens of propaganda. Our mission, therefore, is to confront ignorance with knowledge, bigotry with tolerance, and isolation with the outstretched hand of generosity. Racism can, will, and must be defeated." – Kofi Annan

"I found this out over the years, that racism is a thinly veiled disguise over economics and money. It really is." – Quincy Jones

"One of the worst things about racism is what it does to young people." – Alvin Ailey

"You don't fight racism, the best way to fight racism is with solidarity." Bobby Seale

"The racism, sexism, I never let it be my problem. It's their problem. If I see a door comin' my way, I'm knockin' it down. And if I can't knock down the door, I'm sliding through the window. I'll never let it stop me from what I wanna do." - Rosie Perez

"I was raised to believe that excellence is the best deterrent to racism or sexism. And that's how I operate my life." – Oprah Winfrey

"We may have different religions, different languages, different colored skin, but we all belong to one human race." – Kofi Annan

"The peoples of earth are one family." – Ruth Fulton Benedict

"The love of one's country is a splendid thing, but why should love stop at the border?" – Pablo Casals

"We are eternally linked not just to each other but our environment."
– Herbie Hancock

"We cannot afford to be separate... we have to see that all of us are in the same boat." - Dorothy Height

"Our prime purpose in this life is to help others. And if you can't help them, at least don't hurt them." - Dalai Lama

Love lives in palaces as well as in thatched cottages." – Japanese Proverb

Racism is a refuge for the ignorant. It seeks to divide and to destroy. It is the enemy of freedom, and deserves to be met head-on and stamped out."
– Pierre Berton

"To live anywhere in the world today and be against equality because of race or color is like living in Alaska and being against snow." – William Faulkner

"Love all, trust a few, do wrong to none." – William Shakespeare

A NOTE FROM THE AUTHOR...

My hopes are that you find this book to be enjoyable and that it makes you at least ponder on the fact that we really are all one. I believe we are all in the same boat. Metaphorically, we are at the front, back, or middle, but still on the same boat.

Laughter, tears, joy, pain, trials and tribulations. Change is inevitable. Let us all enjoy the ride, and appreciate this thing called life because it is truly a gift of love.